Waldo's Christmas Surprise

Written and illustrated by
Hans Wilhelm

RANDOM HOUSE
Happy House Group

It was two days before Christmas. Harry, Cornelius, Monty, and I were busy building a snowman when Fritz appeared with his little niece Emily and introduced her.

"Emily is from the South and has never seen snow before," Fritz told us. "She doesn't know much about our winters."

It turned out Emily also didn't know much about Christmas. "Who is Santa Claus, Waldo?" she asked me, shivering in the cold air.

"Santa Claus," I explained, "brings presents and toys to human children at Christmas time."

"Does he also bring presents to animal children?" Emily asked.

"Well," I said, "he hasn't been around this part of the forest for many years. I guess he is too busy visiting all the human children to have much time left for animals."

"Do you think he will come if I write to him?" Emily asked.

"I don't think so," said Monty. "I've never seen him, myself."

"Neither have I," Harry added, shaking his head.

"You see, Santa Claus is only for human children," Fritz said to Emily. "So forget about the whole idea. Let's go home now before you catch a cold."

Early the next morning I saw Emily pulling Fritz toward the mailbox.

"I wrote a letter to Santa Claus," she said, waving a large envelope, "and I asked him to come and bring me a present!"

"Good luck!" I said. "But don't get your hopes up too high. I don't want you to be disappointed if he doesn't come."

"He will—you'll see!" Emily cried.

Poor Emily, I thought. Christmas Day was tomorrow. She was setting herself up for a big disappointment, I was sure.

Suddenly I had an idea. If Emily wanted to see Santa, she would, I decided.

I quickly went into
town and bought a few
things for a surprise. I
was very pleased with my
idea and could hardly
wait to see Emily's eyes
on Christmas morning!

The next day I got
up very early to get
ready. I put on the
red Santa Claus suit
that I had bought.

I looked at myself
in the mirror. I was
delighted! Even my
own mother wouldn't
have recognized me.

I put on my boots
and tried out a few
*Ho, ho, ho*s. Then off
I went, carrying a
present for Emily.

When I was near Fritz's house, I noticed many other tracks in the snow leading to his front door.

I guess Fritz is having a big Christmas party. It's strange that I didn't get an invitation, I thought. But today is Christmas, and Santa is always welcome on a day like this!

Then I knocked.

I could hear little Emily's footsteps coming to the door.

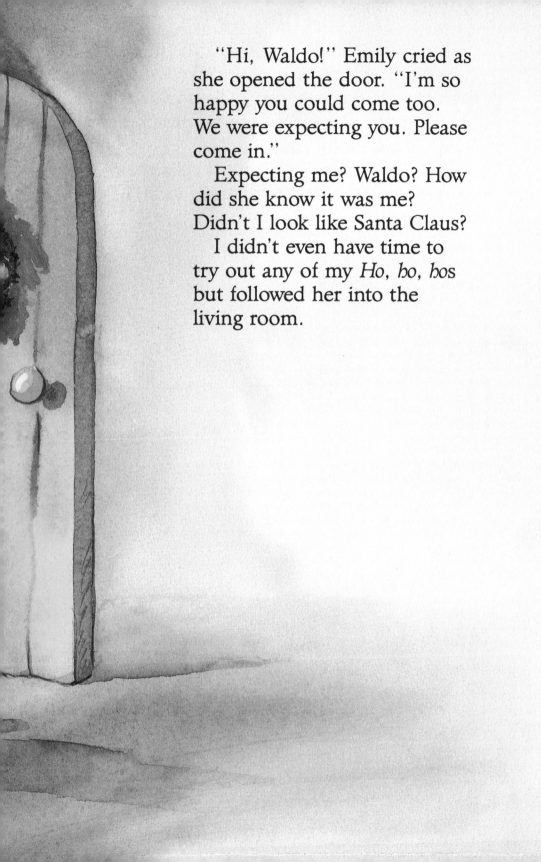

"Hi, Waldo!" Emily cried as she opened the door. "I'm so happy you could come too. We were expecting you. Please come in."

Expecting me? Waldo? How did she know it was me? Didn't I look like Santa Claus?

I didn't even have time to try out any of my *Ho, ho, hos* but followed her into the living room.

There were Fritz, Monty, Cornelius, and Harry, sitting on the sofa and having tea. And each one was dressed up as Santa Claus!

"We didn't want Emily to be disappointed!" Monty explained.

"I know, I know!" I said. "I thought of the same surprise. Merry Christmas to all of you!"

Soon Emily opened all her presents. There was a beautiful jacket from Fritz, a pair of warm winter pants from Monty, a woolen cap from Harry, and mittens from Cornelius.

Then Emily opened my gift. "Oh, red boots—my favorite color!" she said happily. "Let's all go outside and play in the snow. I won't be cold now!" she added.

Suddenly there was a loud
knock at the door.
"Who could that be?"
asked Fritz. "Everybody is
here already."
We cautiously went to
the door.

But by the time Fritz opened the door, the visitor had already left. We could see the back of his sleigh disappearing behind the snow-covered tops of the fir trees.

"Santa Claus!" called Emily as loud as she could.

But all we heard was a faint "Ho, ho, ho!"

"Look, he brought me a present!" Emily said. She pointed to a beautiful red sled. Hanging from it was a label that read FOR EMILY FROM SANTA CLAUS.

"I knew he would come! I knew it!" cried Emily as she danced around her new sled.

    This was certainly one of the best Christmas
Days we had ever had! And Emily enjoyed
riding on her special sled—pulled by five
Santa Clauses!